THE SECRET SATURDAYS

CARTOON NETWORK.

VENGEANCE OF THE HIBAGON

Adapted by I. Trimble
Illustrated by Scott Jeralds

A STEPPING STONE BOOK™
Random House 🏠 New York

Visit us on the Web! www.randomhouse.com/kids

Educators and librarians for a variety of teaching tools, visit us at www.randomhouse.com/teachers

Library of Congress Cataloging-in-Publication Data
Trimble, Irene.
Vengeance of the Hibagon / adapted by I. Trimble ; illustrated by Scott Jeralds. — 1st. ed.
p. cm.
ISBN 978-0-375-86428-5 (trade)—978-0-375-96428-2 (library binding)
I. Jeralds, Scott. II. Secret Saturdays (Television program). III. Title.
PZ7.T735185Ven 2009
[Fic]—dc22
2009005108

www.randomhouse.com/kids
Printed in the United States of America
10 9 8 7 6 5 4 3 2 1

Chapter 1

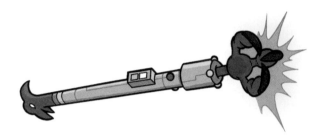

In a state-of-the-art secret laboratory off the coast of Japan, Professor Taro Mizuki proudly stood next to his latest—and possibly greatest—invention. Mizuki hoped his amazing new discovery would change the world. And he was very excited to be presenting the invention to his benefactor via videophone.

Shoji Fuzen was a very wealthy Japanese businessman—and very secretive. He rarely appeared anywhere in person. Even being part

of a teleconference with him was a great honor.

"The tiger!" Mizuki exclaimed, pointing to the huge cat in midleap above his head. "One of nature's most ferocious killers! So dangerous, we cryogenically froze this one to keep ourselves safe from attack."

"The demonstration, please, Professor Mizuki," Fuzen said from the videophone monitor. Two of Fuzen's dark-suited bodyguards stood in the room with Mizuki. Their presence reminded the professor that Fuzen was strictly business.

"Yes, yes, of course," Mizuki said quickly.

The guards listened, stone-faced, as Mizuki apologized. "Forgive my theatrics," he said, bowing. "I'm just so grateful for your generous support of this project."

Shoji Fuzen nodded. "Please continue."

Mizuki lifted a large laser device. He pointed it at the tiger and turned on the power. Glowing beams of blue light surrounded the wild creature.

"Shoji Fuzen," Mizuki announced, "I give you the fiercest beast in the jungle!"

The tiger suddenly sprang to life. It lunged at Professor Mizuki with the force of a freight train.

Shoji Fuzen gasped, expecting to see the professor being torn to pieces. Instead, the tiger licked Mizuki's face affectionately and barked, "Rrrrufff! Ruff!"

Professor Mizuki patted the tiger and smiled. "From man-eating beast to man's best friend," he said proudly. "I have successfully transferred the brain of a dog into a tiger!"

The tiger curled up at Professor Mizuki's feet.

The professor explained that the dog he had used in the experiment was uninjured. It would simply sleep until he transferred its brain back into its body.

Shoji Fuzen nodded, impressed with the new technology. "Well done, Professor Mizuki."

"No, no," Mizuki said humbly. "It is you who have done well. The dream you funded is now a reality!" Mizuki thought about how many people his invention would help. "With this device, no illness will be terminal, no paralysis permanent!"

Shoji Fuzen had heard enough. He held up his hand. "And no do-gooder professor will bore me to tears," he growled.

Mizuki was confused. "Sir?" he asked.

"You are a very intelligent man, Mizuki," Shoji Fuzen said. Then he grinned. "But you know

nothing of my dreams."

The two men in black suits wheeled in a huge, hairy, frozen creature that looked like a gorilla.

Mizuki was stunned. He suddenly realized how his invention was going to be used. Shoji Fuzen was going to transplant a human brain into the enormous beast!

Mizuki looked at the hideous creature's face and screamed, "No! Nooooo!"

The last word Professor Mizuki heard before his world changed forever was "Hibagon!"

Chapter 2

Meanwhile, a high-tech airship was cruising far above the Pacific Ocean. It belonged to the Saturdays, a family of secret scientists who studied cryptids, strange, exotic creatures that most people thought were just myths and legends—certainly not real! The Saturdays searched the globe, exploring ancient ruins, dark forests, darker caves, and anyplace else where these unusual beasts might be found.

Once a cryptid was discovered and cataloged,

the Saturdays made sure the creature's existence was kept a secret. It was their job to protect the cryptid from the world—and in some cases, to protect the world from the cryptid's unusual powers.

At the moment, Doc Saturday, supergenius and head of the Saturday family, was busy studying a fragment of the broken Kur Stone. It was the only clue he had to the whereabouts of an ancient Sumerian cryptid called Kur. According to legend, whoever controlled Kur would possess a nearly limitless source of power. Doc had to find Kur before his archenemy, the evil madman V. V. Argost, did.

Doc had been examining his piece of the stone nonstop for days. Argost already had the other two pieces. The race was on, and the fate

of the whole world was at stake.

"There, you see?" Doc said, pointing to a tiny mark on the stone. His wife, Drew, looked over his shoulder.

"When I enlarge the projection of our Kur Stone piece one hundred times," Doc said, "you see a chip in the surface. What does that tell you?"

"That it's a very old rock?" Drew replied, raising an eyebrow. "You've been studying that thing too long, Doc. I think you're seeing things. Take a break."

She was worried. Even supergeniuses needed their rest.

On the other side of the control room, their son, eleven-year-old Zak Saturday, had his nose buried in a book about Sumerian writing. Hidden inside the book was a magazine devoted to his favorite TV show, *V. V. Argost's Weirdworld.*

Zak was a huge fan. He knew Argost was his dad's archenemy, but Argost also happened to have the coolest show on television. Each week, Argost presented cryptids that were weirder and wilder than any Zak had ever seen— and he had seen plenty!

Zak had a special bond with cryptids. He could calm—and sometimes even control— them. But he was still working out the kinks in his cryptid-influencing powers. He knew he might have to face Kur someday, so he got in as much practice as he could.

Zak's pet, Komodo, was busy turning the pages of the magazine with his sticky tongue. Komodo was the cryptid version of a Komodo dragon. He could camouflage himself to become nearly invisible.

A seven-foot-tall gorilla-cat named Fiskerton was looking at the magazine over Zak's shoulder. Fiskerton was one of the last of the legendary Fiskerton Phantoms. He was more like a brother than a pet.

Zon, on the other hand, was a little wilder and would never quite be tame. But at the moment, the leathery-winged pterosaur was content to look out the airship's window as it floated through the clouds.

Zak suddenly sniffed the air. A bad smell was coming from his dad's direction.

"How about a shower?" Zak teased Doc. Zak understood that his dad was working hard, but this particular body-odor experiment had gone on much longer than necessary.

Fiskerton looked Doc's way and held his nose.

Doc sniffed his own armpit and shrugged. He had more important things on his mind. "The Kur Stone is our only hope for figuring out Argost's next move," he told his family. "There's no time to waste, not even for personal hygiene!"

Zak rolled his eyes. He knew he'd never get away with a line like that.

Drew placed a hand on Doc's shoulder. "Hey, big man," she said. "We all want to stop Argost. We'll figure this thing out, but not by letting it take over our lives. You need rest and food."

Doc nodded, but he wasn't really listening.

Drew grabbed a hairbrush and ran it through Fiskerton's long, furry coat. She removed the loose fur from the brush and slapped it between two pieces of bread from a loaf on the table.

"This should wake him up," she whispered to Zak as she handed Doc the sandwich. The family watched in amazement as Doc took a bite and swallowed.

Just then, the ship's communicator chimed. "Maybe that's Doc's stomach calling his brain," Drew said, going to answer the call herself.

"Dad, seriously, you need a break," Zak suggested. "Maybe we could go a few rounds in the minigym?"

Zak pulled the Claw from his belt. The Claw was a very special weapon Doc had made for Zak. It looked like a stick, but at one end was an ancient artifact called the Hand of Tsul'Kalu. It helped Zak focus his ability to subdue cryptids. Doc had also added a few cool features to the weapon so that Zak could use it as a fighting staff, a vaulting pole, and a grappling hook.

"You know?" Zak told him. "My Claw versus your Battle Glove?"

The Claw glowed a little, as though it understood that it might get a workout.

"You could help me with my cryptid powers," Zak said, still trying to draw his father away from the lab.

Doc began to look annoyed. "Zak," he said finally, "this is important."

Zak sighed. Fiskerton grumbled.

"Promise me," Zak said to the big gorilla-cat, "if I ever go superobsessive about something, you'll snap me out of it before I eat a hairball sandwich."

Suddenly, the airship veered sharply.

"We just got a call from Dr. Yoshiko," Drew said, returning from the helm. "There's trouble in Japan. Looks like we're going to have to forget about Argost for a while."

Doc was not happy. "What!" he shouted. "Is it really *that* important?"

"It's our kind of trouble," she replied.

Doc nodded. And to everyone's relief, finally headed for the shower.

Chapter 3

In a park near the city of Hiroshima, a thug was running through the brush in a panic. A huge, hairy beast was chasing him. It was so close, the thug could hear the beast panting behind him.

A grove of trees suddenly blocked the thug's way. He stopped short and screamed. Then he saw a drainage tunnel on the hillside, and he climbed in as the beast crashed though the trees.

The beast looked into the tunnel, but he was too big to follow the man. Angry that he had lost his prey, the creature threw his head back and howled into the night.

It was the Hibagon from Mizuki's lab, and he was on the loose.

Later that same morning, the Saturdays stepped onto the crowded streets of Hiroshima. Doc looked around at the hundreds of vendors and at the billboards flashing overhead.

"This," Doc said, "is supposed to make me stop thinking about Argost?"

Every street vendor was selling *V. V. Argost's Weirdworld* T-shirts, posters, and mugs. Argost's

creepy pale face peered out at them from every direction.

"Japan is *Weirdworld*'s number-one fan base," Zak said. Then he remembered he wasn't supposed to know anything about *Weirdworld*. He gulped and added quickly, "Uh, that's what I hear. You know, on the streets, when I'm fighting evil."

Doc waved a hand at all the merchandise. There was even a V. V. Argost energy drink. "Look at this garbage," Doc scoffed. "How can so many people fall for that lunatic's act?"

Zak shrugged. He knew Argost wanted to take over the world, but the TV show was so good. Every week, Argost went to lost and forbidden places. He even had an evil assistant named Munya who could change his DNA and become half spider, half man! What could top that?

Zak put on his most innocent face. "I guess their lives are just so very empty," he said, shaking his head. "I'm going to take a moment to be sad for all those Argost fans."

As soon as his parents weren't looking, Zak snuck away and rushed up to a street vendor. "How much for the talking Argost figure?" he asked slyly.

"Give me twenty dollars," the vendor demanded.

Zak tried to haggle but was unable to get the price down. He put the money in the vendor's hand and stuffed the talking Argost figure into his backpack. Then he ran to catch up to his family.

"All right," Doc said, checking out the block. "We'll take a quick look around, but if we don't see anything soon, we should head back. We've got more important work to do."

Suddenly, out of nowhere, the panicked thug came running down the street and knocked Drew over. Zak waved his fist at the guy and yelled something in Japanese that made everyone in the crowd blush.

"I really wish I hadn't taught you that word," Drew said to Zak as Doc helped her up.

Just then, a roar echoed through the street. The massive gorillalike Hibagon was charging at them! He smashed everything in his way.

"Whoa!" Zak said, amazed by the beast's size and strength.

Fiskerton made a muscle with his own arm to compare to the Hibagon's. Zak nudged him with an elbow. "You could take him," Zak said, trying to cheer up his friend.

"Zak," Doc said, pointing to the Hibagon. "See if you can calm him down."

Zak took the Claw from his belt. "Use cryptid powers on the big guy," he replied. "Got it!"

The Saturdays chased the beast into a dead-end alley. The Hibagon had the thug cornered.

The thug scrambled to climb the brick wall behind him. The creature grabbed the screaming man and pressed him up against it.

"He has a shipment coming into Tokyo Harbor tonight!" the terrified thug cried, telling the Hibagon what he wanted to know. "He'll be there, I swear! Please, just let me live!"

Just then, someone tapped the Hibagon on the shoulder. It was Zak, holding the Claw. Drew and Doc stood by with their weapons drawn.

Zak focused all his mental energy on the creature, and the Claw began to glow. "Good gorilla," Zak said softly. "Now, let's put the dirty, rude man back down, okay?"

The Hibagon snorted and knocked the Claw off his massive shoulder. He dropped the thug and vaulted over the wall.

"He didn't even flinch," Zak said, disappointed that his powers hadn't worked. "That's never happened before!"

Doc patted Zak on the shoulder. "Let's find out why," he suggested.

Fiskerton lifted Zak onto his shoulders, and the Saturdays quickly took off after the beast.

Chapter 4

The Hibagon was tearing through the streets of Hiroshima with the Saturdays on his heels. Drew pulled out her Cortex Disrupter. It was capable of temporarily scrambling the brain function of just about any living thing.

Drew aimed the Cortex Disrupter at the Hibagon's back. But just as she was about to fire, Doc stopped her.

"Too many pedestrians," Doc said. "Wait until

he moves to a less populated area."

"That may not be anytime soon," Zak said as he watched the Hibagon approach a crowded bullet-train station.

The beast barreled onto the train platform, sending passengers screaming out of his way. He raced across the tracks, nimbly dodging a speeding train. Then the Hibagon crossed several more sets of tracks and leapt onto another platform. The Saturdays knew they had to follow, but the trains were moving at 150 miles per hour!

The Saturdays jumped onto the roof of a passing train. Then they made a daring leap onto a train going in the other direction. Hopping from train to train, they crossed to the opposite platform.

Zak aimed the Claw at the Hibagon again. This time, the Claw shot out a cable and snagged the Hibagon's furry shoulder. The creature ran, pulling Zak on his heels like a water-skier behind a speedboat.

"Whoa!" Zak shouted as he leaned to one side to avoid smashing into a lamppost.

The Hibagon turned and tore the Claw off his shoulder. He snapped the cable like a bullwhip. The force sent Zak falling backward onto the train tracks.

"Zak!" Drew shouted. A bullet train zoomed toward her son.

Doc, Drew, and Fiskerton watched in horror as the speeding train roared past. In a flash, it was gone—and so was Zak.

Then Zak swung down from some pipes

overhead, doing a perfect flip onto the tracks. His hair was a little mussed, but he was fine. "Whoo-hoo!" he yelled, feeling pretty pleased with himself.

Doc and Drew pulled him onto the train platform.

"That was incredibly dangerous," Drew said, hugging him.

"Mom," Zak told her. "You're the one who taught me that move."

"I know," she said, almost in tears. "I'm just so proud you nailed it."

Fiskerton growled and pointed to the bridge above the tracks. The Hibagon was looking down at them. "If you value your life, you will pursue me no further," he said. Then the beast reached out, grabbed the roof of a speeding train, and disappeared into the distance in seconds.

The Saturdays were stunned at hearing the creature speak.

"Did the giant gorilla thing just use the word 'pursue'?" Zak asked.

The Saturdays returned to their airship. Drew wanted to follow the bullet train and get some facts on the creature from the Cryptopedia. This was a device that contained information on every known cryptid. It could also supply the myths and legends that surrounded many of the unknown ones.

Zak plugged his Cryptopedia into the console. He downloaded the information. In just a matter

of seconds, he saw that he had a match.

"'Hibagon: from the Mount Hiba region of Japan,'" he read aloud. He frowned. "It's definitely a cryptid. So what happened to my powers?"

Drew shook her head. "I'm not sure, Zak. We don't usually see that kind of intelligence in a cryptid."

Komodo hissed at the insult. Fiskerton put his hands over his face and groaned.

"I'm sure she meant *other* cryptids," Zak told them. But Fiskerton and Komodo still left the control room in a huff.

"Maybe your dad's run into something like this before," Drew said, looking around for Doc. "Where is he, anyway?" She pushed the intercom button for the lab and yelled, "Doc!"

In the lab, Doc jumped at the sound of his

wife's voice. He was staring at the Kur Stone.

"I thought we were putting Argost aside," she told him.

Zak couldn't help smiling. "Hey, Dad," he said into the speaker, "you want some pointers on how not to get busted for stuff you're not supposed to be doing?"

Just then, Komodo walked back into the room with Zak's *Weirdworld* magazine in his mouth. Zak cringed. *Busted*, he thought as the dragon spit it out. Komodo stuck out his tongue at Zak.

Zak's face turned a dark shade of red. "She's the one who called you dumb!" he shouted to Komodo. "Not me!"

Drew ignored the magazine. "Darling," she said to her husband over the intercom, "could you please focus at least some of that massive brainpower on the problem at hand?"

Zak looked out the ship's window. The bullet train had stopped on the tracks. They could see a trail of broken trees leading to the Pacific coast. "I think he's found his stop," Drew said.

"He's going to Tokyo Harbor," Zak told his dad over the speaker. "Looks like gorilla man is swimming the rest of the way."

Chapter 5

That night at a dock in Tokyo Harbor, workers were unloading a ship with the words FUZEN IMPORTS on its hull. Out of the calm water, the massive Hibagon burst to the surface. He shook his furry head dry. Then, with one long arm, the creature pulled his massive body onto the dock. He looked in the direction of the ship—

Suddenly, a blinding light flashed into the Hibagon's eyes. A huge cargo net spread out and

fell over his body and cinched him tight.

The Saturdays stepped forward and got their first good look at the trapped Hibagon. The simian creature was more than eighteen feet tall and covered in dark gray fur. And at the moment, his eyes were filled with rage.

"Hi there," Drew said, stepping toward the thrashing beast. "If you can speak, I'm guessing you can reason as well. So let's be reasonable."

The furious Hibagon calmed down a little.

"I have nothing to say to the lackeys of Shoji Fuzen," the Hibagon snarled. "Tell your master my vengeance will not be stopped so easily."

"*Ookaay,*" Zak said to the beast. "We'll be sure to do that just as soon as you tell us who Shoji Fuzen is."

"What?" the Hibagon asked, confused. "He

didn't send you to track me?"

But before the Saturdays could answer, a blaster shot hit the Cortex Disrupter in Doc's hand. Then a group of Shoji Fuzen's bodyguards stormed down the dock toward them.

Shoji Fuzen watched the scene from a safe distance on the ship. "Bring me the Hibagon alive and unharmed!" His voice boomed over a loud-speaker to the bodyguards. "Do with the others as you wish."

Doc was familiar with Fuzen's reputation. He posed as a businessman, but he was really Japan's most ruthless crime boss.

The Hibagon shook his shaggy head sadly. "Yes, I have escaped his men once before. You will need me in this fight."

Doc realized the creature was right, and he

gave an approving nod to his wife.

Drew pulled her Tibetan Fire Sword from the scabbard on her back. As moonlight hit the sword, it ignited into a blue flame. She quickly swung the flaming sword at the cargo netting and cut the Hibagon loose.

The Hibagon landed on all fours and let out a ferocious howl. The guards on the ship's upper deck fired their blasters.

Zak fought the oncoming guards back with his Claw. Drew swung her Fire Sword, knocking them into the bay. Doc charged up the kinetic boost on his Battle Glove. The weapon had several different functions, but its punch-enhancing power was its most potent.

Doc threw a punch at one of the guards with his gloved fist, but the man was armed with a steel glove employing similar technology. When Doc's and the guard's gloves connected, the opposing force sent them both flying backward. Doc crashed into Fiskerton. The gorilla-cat fell heavily on top of Doc.

Doc got a big wad of Fiskerton's fur in his mouth. He couldn't quite figure out why it tasted so familiar. But more guards were coming, and there was no time to wonder.

The Hibagon angrily pounded the dock with both his fists. The resulting shock wave threw the guards into the harbor.

Zak got an idea. "Think you can do that again?" he asked.

The big creature nodded.

Zak and Komodo ran to the end of the dock. Zak gave the Hibagon the signal and the creature pounded hard.

The force launched Zak and Komodo into the air. They landed on the ship's upper deck. Zak and Komodo quickly took out the guards who were firing down on Doc and Drew.

With his bodyguards gone, Shoji Fuzen ran for his waiting helicopter. Suddenly, Fuzen grabbed his leg and yelled out in pain!

Komodo decamouflaged. His mouth was tightly clamped onto Fuzen's leg. Shoji Fuzen limped to the helicopter, dragging Komodo behind him, and jumped in.

As the helicopter rose, Fuzen finally shook Komodo loose. Then the helicopter disappeared into the night.

Chapter 6

Zak dove and caught Komodo before the dragon hit the deck. But as he leapt, the talking Argost figure fell from his backpack. "Greetings and *bienvenue,*" the figure said in Argost's sinister voice. "Welcome to *Weirdworld.*"

Zak gasped. "Busted again!"

From the dock below, his mom yelled, "What was that?" But at that moment, a guard was running up behind her. He was holding an oil barrel over his head, about to hurl it at her.

"Behind you!" Zak shouted.

Drew turned and swung her Fire Sword at the barrel, slicing it in two. The barrel halves burst into fireballs. The ship's deck was engulfed in flames.

Zak leapt from the burning ship with Komodo in his arms. He landed next to Doc, Drew, Fiskerton, and the Hibagon. A series of explosions tore through Shoji Fuzen's ship. The ship was sinking. The fight was over.

"Wow," Zak said to the Hibagon. "That Shoji Fuzen was kind of a jerk."

The Hibagon grunted and turned to walk away. Doc grabbed the creature's arm to stop him.

"Get your hands off me," the Hibagon growled.

Doc held on. "We could have handed you over to Fuzen, but we trusted you," Doc told the creature. "Now it's time for you to trust us. Who are you?"

The Hibagon dropped his head. "My name is Professor Taro Mizuki," he said sadly. "At least, it used to be. My research was funded by Shoji Fuzen. I didn't know it, but he turned out to be Tokyo's biggest crime lord."

Mizuki told the Saturdays about the day Shoji Fuzen's men had wheeled the frozen Hibagon into his lab. He remembered Fuzen saying, "Imagine what it can do with the brain of a perfectly honed fighter, ready to answer my every command!"

"I begged him not to do it," Mizuki told Doc. "I told him I had created my transfer device to help people. I would not have it used for evil. But

it became obvious that Fuzen would not listen to reason. I knew there was only one way to stop Fuzen's plan—and that was to take the Hibagon body myself."

As Zak listened, he suddenly understood why his cryptid-influencing powers hadn't worked. The Hibagon's brain was human, not cryptid! Zak felt a lot better. He gave the Claw a loving pat, and a little shake of triumph.

"I stopped them, but the fire destroyed my lab and my human body," Mizuki explained. "Now I am doomed to live out my life as this beast."

Zak looked at the Hibagon's huge body. He thought it would be pretty cool to be eighteen feet tall and have superhuman strength and agility.

The Hibagon sighed. "At least I am not without purpose," he told them. "I will take my revenge on the man who did this to me."

"Professor Mizuki, you have our sympathies," Doc said. "But we can't let you take the kind of revenge you have in mind."

"I will not let Fuzen just walk away from this!" he bellowed.

"Then don't," Drew told him, indicating the noise of the approaching police sirens. "It sounds like half the Tokyo police force is on its way here. How much illegal merchandise do you think they will find in that big boat with Fuzen's name on it?"

"Let the police do their work," Doc told Mizuki. "If you try it your way, people might get hurt."

Mizuki thought about it. Finally, he said, "Yes. Let Fuzen rot in prison for the rest of his life."

"That's the spirit!" Zak said, patting the Hibagon's furry back.

Mizuki sighed. "It seems I am now a creature without a purpose," he said. "If you will excuse me, I would like some time alone with my thoughts."

Chapter 7

The Hibagon slipped into the shadows. All seemed well, but Doc was not happy with how things had turned out. "A day and a half here, and all we did was keep the good guy from stopping the bad guy," he grumbled.

Doc shook his head angrily. "Argost couldn't have planned this any better!" he said, still obsessing about the Kur Stone. "We just gave our archenemy a massive head start. I can practically hear him laughing at our incompetence!"

Just then, a faint evil laugh came from Zak's backpack. It was the Argost action figure. Doc was stunned and said, "Tell me I'm not the only one hearing that."

Drew looked at Zak's backpack and said, "Unfortunately, no." She unzipped it and pulled out the talking piece of plastic.

Zak gulped. "I was trying to keep it out of the hands of impressionable kids?" he explained. His parents were not amused.

"Doc, what are we going to do about this?" Drew asked.

Doc pulled out his wallet. "I'll give you five hundred dollars cash for it right now," he said.

"Doc!" Drew said, completely surprised.

"Make it six hundred and I'll throw in the

bonus DVD!" Zak said excitedly, pushing his luck.

Doc glared at him.

"*Rrright . . . ,*" Zak said. "Five for the big guy. But why do you want it so bad?"

Moments later, Doc blasted the Argost figure into hundreds of pieces with his Battle Glove.

"Feel better now?" Drew asked Doc.

"I do!" Zak said, jumping up and down. "That was awesome! C'mon, let's blow something else up! Think of how much better you'll feel."

Doc put his hand on Zak's shoulder. "It's not that easy, Zak," he said, suddenly suspicious. "Come to think of it, it never is. If you ask me, the Hibagon gave up his revenge a little too easily."

Doc's instincts were right. Mizuki hadn't given up. Across town, Shoji Fuzen's helicopter was landing on the roof of his forty-story office building. Below him, the Hibagon began climbing up the side of the glass and steel skyscraper.

The crime lord was lucky that Doc had decided to track him down. As the unforgiving Mizuki made his way up the building, the Saturdays flew into Tokyo.

"Okay," Doc said, "we're locked onto Fuzen's DNA signature from that bite Komodo took out of his leg."

Komodo wagged his tail as Zak patted him on the head. "Way to take a bite out of crime, Komodo!"

Doc followed the signal to a tall building.

"We're close," he said. "It should be right about here."

"Whoa!" Zak exclaimed, looking out the airship window. The Hibagon was nearly at the top of Fuzen's building.

"Guess Mizuki's vengeance wasn't so easy to put aside after all," Drew said to Doc.

Chapter 8

Inside his high-rise office, Shoji Fuzen was working at his desk. As he looked out at the Tokyo skyline, the window suddenly shattered into a million shards of glass.

Shoji Fuzen gasped and jumped to his feet. He backed away from his desk and screamed as a huge hairy fist reached through the window.

"'Terrifying creature' were your exact words, I believe," the Hibagon said, seeing the fear in Shoji Fuzen's eyes. The huge beast grabbed

Fuzen and pulled him out the broken window. He stood on the ledge and dangled Fuzen forty stories above the city. "Remember," Mizuki told the crime lord, "you made this happen."

"Put him down, Mizuki!" Drew shouted as she and Doc reached the rooftop.

"A very poor choice of words," Mizuki answered. He opened his huge hand and let Fuzen fall.

Zon suddenly swooped in. Zak jumped on the flying cryptid's back and flew underneath Fuzen.

"Hi," Zak said as he caught the bad man in midair. "You're going to jail!"

Fuzen looked into the blue face of Zak's pterosaur and fainted.

Zon landed on a nearby rooftop. As she unloaded Fuzen, Zak patted the cryptid's neck.

"Nice work, girl!" Zak said to her.

Zon suddenly squawked in alarm. Zak turned to see the Hibagon leaping from Fuzen's building. The creature began to climb toward the rooftop of the building Zak was standing on. Mizuki wasn't going to give up on his revenge until Fuzen was finished!

Zon took off, dive-bombing the huge beast. Mizuki batted her away, sending her crashing through a skyscraper window.

"Zon!" Zak yelled.

The pterosaur stuck her head out the window and squawked. She was okay.

"Go back to the airship!" Zak shouted to her. "It's too dangerous here for you."

With a terrible roar, the Hibagon reached Zak's rooftop.

"It's too dangerous for all of us," Zak said, staring into the furious simian face.

From Fuzen's building, Doc yelled, "Zak! Throw me Fuzen! He's all that Mizuki is after!"

Zak latched his Claw's cable onto Fuzen. He swung Fuzen across the forty-story gap. Doc caught the man's limp body on the other side.

Zak ducked out of the charging Hibagon's way. The huge beast was looking for a way back to Fuzen's building. He began to climb a tall lightning rod.

As the Hibagon reached the very top, the lightning rod tipped over. The creature landed right in the path of Doc and Fuzen.

Mizuki was going after anyone who was holding Fuzen. The Saturdays tossed Fuzen back and forth to each other, trying to keep him out of the Hibagon's massive hands. It was a dangerous game of keep-away.

Zak was about to toss Fuzen to Doc when the Hibagon caught up.

With nowhere to turn, Zak hoisted Fuzen onto his shoulders. He saw a communications tower on top of the building and started to climb.

The Hibagon reached out his long arm and grabbed Zak's foot. Zak struggled to hold on to the tower as the Hibagon pulled him down.

Just then, Fiskerton tackled the Hibagon off the tower. The two apes rolled and tumbled. The cryptids swung around the steel structure, taking swipes at each other with both their hands and their feet.

Above them, Zak kept climbing the tower with Fuzen on his back.

"What's happening? Where am I?" the crime boss suddenly demanded.

Fuzen began to struggle. "Look," Zak explained. "You're a jerk, but I'm trying to save you."

"I can save myself!" Fuzen yelled, twisting out of Zak's grip.

Zak watched him fall right into the hands of the Hibagon.

"No, don't!" Fuzen screamed as the Hibagon slammed him against a fire door. Fuzen was knocked unconscious again.

Zak climbed down the tower as Doc and Drew quickly made their way to the rooftop. The Saturdays surrounded the Hibagon.

"Don't come any closer," Mizuki growled. "It's over. Especially for Shoji Fuzen."

Doc took a step forward. "Professor, don't do this!" he pleaded.

"He took everything from me!" Mizuki howled. "He made me a monster!"

"I know you swore to take revenge on this man," Doc said, thinking of Argost. "I know you're obsessed with stopping him. I know it's all you can think of. I've been there."

Mizuki looked at Doc through his cryptid eyes. He sensed that Doc really understood. "Nothing good can come of obsession, even if the cause is just," Doc told him. "Shoji Fuzen may have taken your human form, but only you decide whether or not you're a monster."

Mizuki knew Doc was right. He released Fuzen, who slid to the floor. "Take him," Mizuki said.

Doc quickly bound Fuzen's wrists. "I hope the

Tokyo Police Department likes them gift-wrapped," he said.

"You know, you're pretty good at this when you actually pay attention," Zak said, looking at his father proudly.

Chapter 9

A few days later, the Saturdays' airship was docked outside a cave on Mount Hiba, Japan. The cave had been fully outfitted with gleaming new lab equipment.

The Hibagon shook Doc's and Drew's hands. "Thank you for saving what was left of the man in me," Mizuki said. "And for providing the means for continuing my research."

"I'm sure you'll have your machine rebuilt in

no time," Doc said confidently.

Zak looked at the Hibagon's massive arms and shoulders.

"And if you're in the market for a body," Zak told him, "I'm willing to talk trade!"

Drew motioned Zak toward the airship and gave him a *don't even think about it* look.

"No, he's not," she said to Mizuki. "But please do stay in touch. You don't have to be alone up here."

Mizuki smiled. He had a surprise to show them.

"I won't be entirely alone," Mizuki said. Then he let out a loud whistle.

The tiger-dog appeared and romped up to the furry Hibagon. It nuzzled Mizuki, sensing its master within the mighty body.

"Whoa!" Zak exclaimed. "That thing is awesome! Can you make me one of those?"

Zak rushed up to greet the tiger-dog. "Hey, guy! Hey, buddy!" he said, petting its black and orange coat. "Can you play fetch? Roll over? Speak?"

The tiger let out a bark that turned into a savage roar. Zak saw its sharp teeth and pulled his hand back.

"You know, I'm cool with the pets I have," he said, smiling meekly.

From the airship, the Saturdays looked out and watched the Hibagon waving goodbye. "Still wondering if this one was important enough?"

Drew asked, teasing her husband.

"Yes, you made your point," Doc replied with a nod. "And without the need for more Fiskerton fur sandwiches."

Drew was a little embarrassed. "Figured that out finally, did you?"

"I deserved it," Doc replied. "I let Argost take over my life. I'm sorry. Although not nearly as sorry as I am for giving Zak five hundred dollars cash."

When Doc looked over at Zak, his son was pulling a life-size talking Argost figure from a huge box. The figure let out an evil laugh.

"It's for target practice," Zak said, hoping his dad would believe him.

"Really?" Doc said with a laugh. "Glad to hear it."

Doc and Zak took the Argost figure to the mini gym. A moment later, the figure exploded into a million pieces.

"Okay!" Zak cried excitedly. "That was definitely worth the five hundred bucks!"

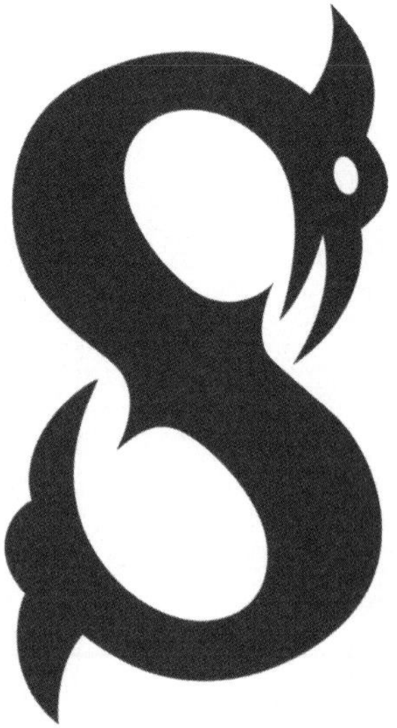